Fairy Ponies

Rainbow Races

Zanna Davidson

Illustrated by Barbara Bongini

Meet the Ponies
Puck
Holly
Bluebell
Pony Queen
Princess Rosabel

Spray
Unicorn Prince
Izagard
Shadow

Fairy Pony Island
Dark Forest
Lake of Gilded Lilies
Tangled Forest
Unicorn Prince's Palace
Enchanted Wood
Dancing Waterfall
Pony Magic School
Magic Pony Pools
Sunlit Sea
Woody Glade

High Mountains
Izagard's House
Rainbow Mountain
Everlasting Rainbow
Summer Palace
Forever Flower Meadow
Rainbow Shore
Butterfly Valley
Silver Stream
Singing River
Meadows
N
W
E
S
Entrance from the Great Oak

Contents

Chapter One

It was a beautiful, moonlit night. Holly crept out of her great-aunt's cottage and down the garden path, her eyes fixed on the oak tree towering ahead of her. When she'd first arrived at Great-Aunt May's house for the summer holidays, Holly had never imagined it would be so full of adventure. But she had discovered another world inside the magical oak tree –

Pony Island, full of beautiful fairy ponies. Last time she'd visited, her friend Puck had promised to show her more of the island. Holly couldn't wait…

She sprinkled herself with magic dust, her stomach fluttering with excitement. Then, as the night sky filled with rainbow sparkles, she felt a tingling, shrinking feeling. Holly closed her eyes as the air whooshed around her, and when she opened them again, she was fairy-sized. Now she was

small enough to enter the oak tree's secret tunnel. She whispered the words of the spell:

"Let me pass into the magic tree,
Where fairy ponies fly wild and free.
Show me the trail of sparkling light,
To Pony Island, shining bright."

Holly ran down the tunnel, filled with delight at the thought of seeing Pony Island again. Reaching for the tiny silver bell around her neck, she rang it until its musical chimes floated ahead of her down the tunnel, letting Puck know she was on her way.

Holly rounded the corner and burst out of the oak tree into a sun-kissed meadow. Puck was already waiting for her, standing knee-deep among the wild flowers with a butterfly resting on his mane. His glossy russet coat gleamed in the sunshine, and his brown eyes twinkled with mischief.

"Come on, Holly!" he said with a grin, fluttering his shimmering wings. "I've got something brilliant to show you."

He crouched down and Holly swung herself onto his back, her fingers tangling in his silky soft mane.

"Where are we going?" she asked, as Puck began beating his wings.

"To Rainbow Shore," Puck replied. "You'll be amazed when you see what's happening there..."

They soared into the azure sky, flying up and up, the warm summer breeze washing over Holly's skin. She breathed in the delicious scent of wild flowers and gazed down at Pony Island, sparkling in the sunlight far away below her.

"Scared?" asked Puck.

"Not any more," Holly replied. This was her third visit to Pony Island, and flying on a fairy pony felt as natural as riding now.

"Look, there's Butterfly Valley," Puck pointed out, as they swooped out of a small wooded glade.

Holly watched in wonder as the valley came alive with butterflies, flitting from flower to flower. Together their shimmering wings made a dazzling patchwork of shining purples, golden yellows and sparkling blues. As she gazed down, Holly thought how lucky she was to be the only human allowed into the secret world of Pony Island.

They passed over little thatched houses and silver streams, until, at last, Rainbow Shore came into view. Holly glimpsed a white beach rolling down to a clear blue sea, where foamy waves frothed and curled along the sand. Then she gasped as she saw a dazzling rainbow, stretching in a glorious arc from far out at sea, across the beach to the foot of a mountain.

"Wow!" cried Holly. "So that's how Rainbow Shore gets its name."

"The rainbow is magical," Puck explained. "It's everlasting. And the mountain it touches is called Rainbow Mountain. Behind it are the rest of the High Mountains. I'd love to go there one day."

Holly stared up at Rainbow Mountain, which reached high above the clouds, as Puck began diving down to the ground. Crowds of fairy ponies were already gathered, with birds hovering above them in the sky, holding a banner, which said *Rainbow Races* in swirling, glittering writing.

Music floated up from the crowd, a jaunty tune played by the Fairy Pony Band with seashell horns and shining silver bells.

Rainbow Races

"What's happening, Puck?" asked Holly. "What are the Rainbow Races?"

Puck simply smiled and nodded to a row of rainbow masts, decorated with ribbons, that were dotted along the shore.

"That's the race course," he explained. "All the racing ponies have to follow the course and there are obstacles along the way. We have to weave in and out of those masts, loop-the-loop above the sand dunes, fly three times around the conch shell and then gallop through the giant sandcastle palace. The winner is the first pony to fly through the rainbow." Puck's eyes were shining with excitement. "The Rainbow Races is the biggest event on the island," he went on. "Fairy ponies travel from far and wide to watch or take part. And this is the first year I'll be old enough to be in one of the races. I'm going to be in the Juniors. I can't wait!" He paused for a moment and looked at her, almost shyly. "Would you like to ride on my back?" he asked.

"Won't I slow you down?" asked Holly. "You'll be the only pony with a rider."

Puck shook his head. "You're as light as a feather," he said. "We can easily win," he added with a grin.

"Then I'd love to!" Holly replied, as excited as Puck at the thought of taking part.

Before she could say more, a fanfare struck up and Holly saw the Fairy Pony Band blowing on their seashell horns. The crowd started cheering, beating their hoofs on the ground in a thunderous round of applause as the Pony Queen flew down through the rainbow, surrounded by a cloak of sparkling stardust, butterflies trailing in her wake. Her butterfly wings shimmered in the sunlight and her creamy white coat was bathed in sunshine.

She came to rest on a raised platform, decked out with garlands of flowers. The Pony Queen smiled down at the crowds and began to speak.

"Welcome to the Rainbow Races,

everyone," she said in her musical voice. "Thank you all for coming..."

But suddenly, the sound of hoofs echoed through the crowd, and Puck and Holly turned their heads to see what was happening. The Pony Queen stiffened, her expression frozen in anger: something was terribly wrong.

Chapter Two

As the crowds parted, Holly saw three huge, dark ponies cantering towards the Pony Queen. She felt a quiver of fear run through her body. She would have recognized those ponies anywhere – Shadow, Storm and Ravenstar – the three most evil ponies on the island.

Shadow was glowering at the Pony Queen.

His coat gleamed blue-black in the sunshine, his huge wings glittering brightly. Behind him followed Storm and Ravenstar, glaring threateningly around them.

"How dare they come back?" fumed Puck. "After they tried to overthrow the Pony Queen. I can't believe it."

"Shhh!" whispered Holly. "Let's hear what they have to say."

Shadow fixed his black eyes on the Pony Queen, his expression filled with scorn.

"Your time is up!" he sneered. "Give up the crown or Pony Island is doomed."

Holly watched the Pony Queen swoop

down from her platform so that she was standing face to face with Shadow and his henchmen.

A group of ponies swiftly gathered around her, and Holly recognized them as the Spell-Keepers – the Pony Queen's closest advisors and the most magical ponies on the island.

"I will never give up my powers," said the Pony Queen. "It is my duty, and my privilege, to protect Pony Island."

As she spoke, the crown of magical flowers she always wore began to glow, casting rays of light around her. Holly thought she looked magnificent as she stood before them, tossing her silken mane.

"This might make you change your mind," Shadow scoffed. "Hold it up," he commanded, and Storm and Ravenstar held aloft a dark wooden casket for everyone to see. The Pony Queen stumbled back in shock.

"Yes! I have the Cloudburst Casket," Shadow laughed. "Prepare to feel its powers."

Some of the fairy ponies gasped in horror, while others looked at each other in confusion. Holly glanced over at Puck and saw the terror on his face. "What's happening?" she asked.

"It can't be true... The Cloudburst Casket?" he whispered. "I thought it only existed in stories."

"What is it?" Holly asked.

"A piece of ancient pony magic," Puck explained. "The old legends say it contains all the storms and rain clouds on Pony Island. They were trapped inside the casket long ago, so the island would always be bright and sunny. I don't know what will happen if Shadow opens it..."

Puck stopped as Shadow began speaking again. His tone was mocking. "You have one chance to surrender peacefully, otherwise I'm going to release the storms from the casket."

"I refuse," said the Pony Queen calmly. "You can't threaten me with the casket.

Besides, I doubt you even know *how* to control it. No one does. Its secrets are locked in the mists of time. You wouldn't dare unleash its powers."

"Wouldn't I?" smirked Shadow.

He leaped over to where Storm and Ravenstar held it aloft, and with a flourish, pulled back the lid of the casket. The Pony Queen raced forwards to stop him, but she was too late. A howling black cloud spilled out of the casket, covering everything in its path. Frozen with fear, the fairy ponies watched as the dark cloud began filling the sky,

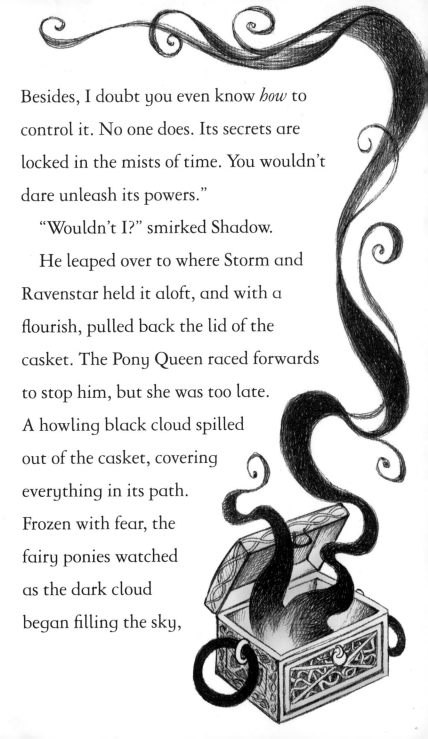

covering the rainbow and blocking its light.

Shadow's deep voice rang out over the piercing shriek of the wind.

"By sunset, the whole of Pony Island will be in darkness," he declared, beating his great wings. "Only I can stop the magic. Unless the Pony Queen gives me her throne before the sun sets, Pony Island will be in darkness for ever."

Chapter Three

The Spell-Keepers moved quickly, rushing to follow Shadow and his guards. They plunged straight into the storm, which was growing fiercer by the second. Holly shivered as she saw how quickly the sparkling blue sky was disappearing beneath the cloud of darkness.

The casket lay abandoned on the ground, its yawning mouth still spilling out the black fog. The Pony Queen stood over it, chanting an ancient, complex spell. At last the casket snapped shut, but it was too late. The evil black cloud had spread across the sky.

A cry from above made everyone look up.

"We've lost them," shouted Snapdragon, one of the Spell-Keepers.

Holly could see that he was fighting hard against the wind as he tried to land, and behind him, the other Spell-Keepers were struggling to keep steady as they followed him out of the storm clouds.

"The wind is too fierce. It kept forcing us back," Snapdragon explained.

The Pony Queen flew onto the platform and turned to face the anxious crowd of fairy ponies.

"Go home, now, all of you," she said. "You need to find shelter before darkness covers the island. The Spell-Keepers and I will work our hardest to catch the storm clouds and reverse the spell, but for your own safety, the Rainbow Races are postponed."

Puck and Holly watched as the rest of the fairy ponies took to the skies, muttering and whispering anxiously, flying low so as to avoid the billowing black clouds.

"Come on, Puck," said Holly, as icy rain began to fall. "Shouldn't we follow the others?"

"Wait a minute," said Puck, seeing the Spell-Keepers had grouped together a little distance from the casket, deep in discussion about what to do next. "Quick, let's take a look at it."

They crept over to where the casket lay. In the fast-fading light, they could just make out the detailed patterns on the sides of the casket. Peering closely, Holly spotted a carving of a spider on the lid.

"What do you think it means?" Holly asked Puck.

"I don't know," Puck said, shaking his head.

"Maybe it's a clue," said Holly, tracing her finger over the casket.

"Maybe..." said Puck, bending even closer.

"What are you two still doing here?" said a concerned voice behind them. Puck jumped; it was his mother, Bluebell, one of the Spell-Keepers. "Didn't you hear the Pony Queen?" she said, an anxious frown on her brow. "It's not safe for you to stay here. I don't want any harm to come to either of you. Puck, please take Holly home before this storm gets any worse."

"But can't we...?" Puck began.

Then he saw his mother's expression and realized she was serious.

"The magic from the Cloudburst Casket is very powerful," Bluebell went on, this time more gently. "It's going to take all our energy to work out how to stop the storm before nightfall. We need to study the ancient spell books. I can't be worrying about what you're up to as well. Please, Puck, take Holly back to the Great Oak. Then go home and wait for me to return."

Reluctantly, Puck turned to Holly, who jumped on his back.

"Come on, Holly," Puck sighed, loud enough for Bluebell to hear. "I'll take you home."

Holly looked down in anguish at Rainbow Shore as Puck took to the sky, flying low to avoid the storm. But as soon as they were cloaked by cloud, Puck made a sudden swerve in direction, flying up into the storm clouds, heading for the High Mountains.

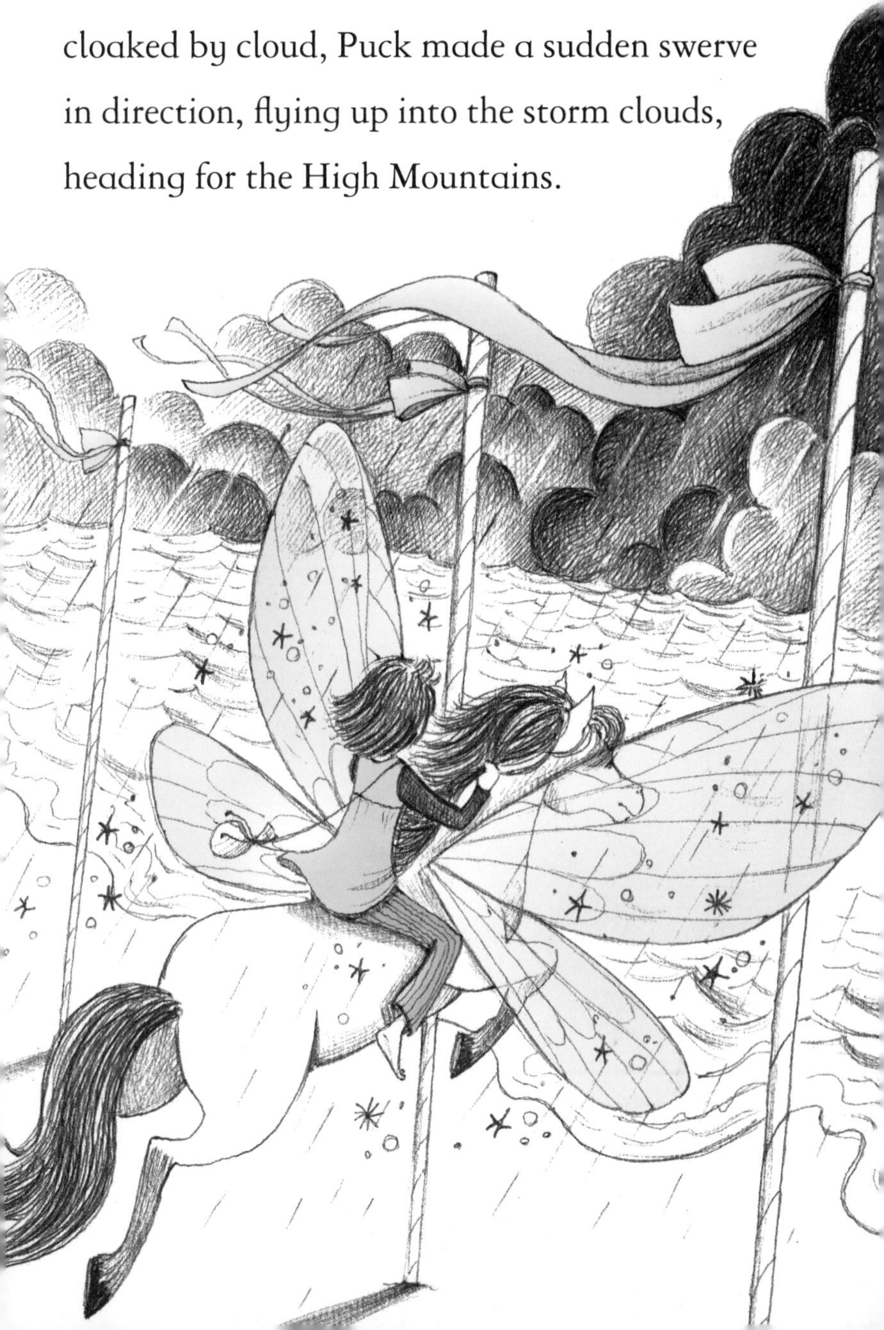

"What are you doing?" cried Holly.

She could feel the wind growing stronger as they flew through the clouds, buffeting them this way and that. Rain lashed against her skin, soaking her pyjamas, and she realized that for the first time on Pony Island, she was bitterly cold. She could feel Puck shivering beneath her as well.

"We can't let Shadow get away with this," Puck said through chattering teeth. "He flew towards the High Mountains. We *must* be able to find him there. I've never been this cold before," he added. "I can't bear it. We've got to get the sunshine back."

"But this is a job for the Spell-Keepers," insisted Holly. "What happens if we get into trouble? They'd have to stop their work to come and rescue us."

"We won't get into trouble," said Puck, confidently. "Besides, we can't wait for the Spell-Keepers to search through those dusty old books. You heard what Shadow said. We only have until the end of the day to stop the storm clouds. We need action!"

Holly looked down through the swirling mists of cloud at what was left of the Rainbow Races – the banners that had fluttered so cheerily in the breeze were rain-soaked and ripped by the gale. The towering sand palace was a sodden lump on the beach and the waves were lashing against the masts in a wind-whipped fury.

Holly knew what they were doing was dangerous – but at the same time, she felt

Puck was right. They had to try and help. She couldn't watch Pony Island be destroyed.

"Come on. Let's find Shadow and stop the casket's magic!"

The higher they flew, the colder the air became. Holly saw her breath coming out in misty gasps. Through the shifting swirls of cloud she could now glimpse icy snow-capped mountains.

"Still no sign of Shadow," said Holly, shouting over the roar of the storm. "Perhaps he's sheltering on the mountainside."

"Maybe," Puck panted. "I'll land on Rainbow Mountain. It's the nearest of the High Mountains."

Puck started swooping down through the cloud, but in the gathering darkness,

it was hard to tell where the cloud ended and the mountain began.

Holly could feel Puck's limbs had grown stiff and frozen. They were both drenched with freezing rain, their bodies shivering from blasts of bitter wind.

"We have to land soon," said Puck, desperately searching for a way through the cloud. "I don't know how much longer I can keep flying for..."

Suddenly there was a clap of thunder, so loud it seemed to ring through Holly's whole body, shaking her to the core.

"That sounded close," she said, trying to

keep her voice light to hide the tremble of fear.

"Too close," said Puck, anxiously looking up.

The next moment the whole sky lit up as a fork of lightning stabbed through the thick black clouds, heading straight for them.

"Watch out!" cried Holly.

Puck began madly flapping his wings, but a second bolt of lightning sent him spinning through the clouds. Holly could only grip tightly onto his mane as they began to plummet through the sky.

Chapter Four

Holly closed her eyes, not wanting to see the ground rushing up to meet them. She felt Puck's mane slipping between her fingers, then, with a soft thud, she realized she had landed.

"Holly!" Puck called. "Are you okay?"

She could hear him, but couldn't see him, even though she was sure he had only landed a little distance beyond her. His voice sounded strangely muffled.

"I'm fine," Holly called back, gingerly moving her limbs.

A moment later, Puck popped up out of the snow beside her.

"We've landed in a snowdrift," Holly realized, gazing around her at the piles of fluffy white snow.

"I know!" said Puck, grinning. "Thank the stars! It must have cushioned our fall."

They stumbled out of the snowdrift, shaking off the snow, both of them shivering in the fierce wind. Holly could hear her teeth chattering like castanets inside her head.

"I'll cast a warming spell," said Puck. "Otherwise we're going to freeze out here."

He came close to Holly and huddled against her:

"Fire sprite, fire bright,
Strike the darkness with your light.
Dance your flames around us here,
Bring us warmth and bring us cheer."

As he finished speaking, a small ring of magical flames lit up the dark sky, surrounding them in a flickering circle of light.

Holly put out her hands, warming them on the dancing flames, smiling as she felt the heat seep into her skin. But no sooner had she dried off, when a howling wind came whipping around the mountainside. In one great gust, it extinguished the flames and left Puck and Holly shivering. In seconds, Holly was numb with cold once more.

"I could try the spell again," said Puck, doubtfully, "but it's not a very powerful one.

I think the storm's too fierce."

"We need to find shelter," Holly replied. "And fast."

She looked up the mountain as she spoke, but the dark clouds hung heavy, obscuring the view.

"Do you have any idea where we are?" she asked Puck.

"No," said Puck, glumly. "None at all."

"Well, let's keep moving," Holly suggested. "At least that will keep us warm."

They began stumbling down the mountain, but it was hard to move through the deep snow.

"What's that?" cried Holly suddenly, peering through the gloom. "I think I see a light ahead. It looks like it's coming from a cottage."

"It can't be," Puck replied. "No one lives on the High Mountains."

"Then it could be Shadow! I think we should investigate," Holly insisted.

Puck nodded in reply.

They trudged on through the snow, a fresh blizzard filling the air with huge white flakes, and making it hard to follow the light.

At last they came to the edge of a thick forest of fir trees. Here, the snow was lighter on the ground, making walking much easier.

"Look! It *is* a cottage. We're saved!" cried Puck, as they wound their way between the trees.

Holly could just make out tumbledown stone walls and a little wooden door beneath a thatched roof sprinkled with snow.

The thought of light and warmth gave them both a boost and they ran the last stretch to the door, rapping on it loudly and calling out for help. But there was no answer.

"It's no use," said Holly at last. "No one's in." She could feel icy snowflakes sliding down the back of her neck, clinging to her skin and soaking her clothes from within. She glanced over at Puck, but he was looking away from her, his gaze directed deep into the forest, his ears pricked.

"What is it?" asked Holly.

"Listen!" said Puck. "I thought I heard something."

Peering through the blizzard, Holly could just make out a large, strange shape heading their way. It had the head of a pony, but its

back was covered in lumps, like some kind of monster.

"Oh no!" cried Puck in fear. "A snow monster!"

Holly wrapped her arms around Puck, clinging to his trembling body as the creature drew closer. Steam poured from its nostrils like an eerie mist and the shadow it cast was huge, looming and menacing…

Chapter Five

"What is it?" Holly whispered, burying her face in Puck's mane.

But as the creature stepped into the light, she couldn't help peering through her fingers. Holly gasped with surprise. It wasn't a monster at all, but a pony, carrying a pile of firewood on its back. He wasn't like any fairy pony Holly had ever seen before. His coat had a strange silver sheen, and his wings looked powerful and heavy. His mane was icy white, long and flowing, and studded with glittering snowflakes.

Puck and Holly stayed frozen to the spot. There was nothing friendly in the pony's expression. His brow was lowered in a threatening frown and his eyes bored into

them. He stalked up to Puck and Holly until he was only inches away from them.

"What are you doing here?" he asked, his voice stern.

Holly could feel Puck quaking with fear. It wasn't the pony's size that was formidable – but his expression. His deep-black eyes looked as if they held years of knowledge, and could wither you with one glance.

Puck opened his mouth to speak, but no words came out. Taking a deep breath, Holly edged her way out from behind Puck to face the pony.

"Please," she began, trying to keep her voice steady, "we don't mean to disturb you, but we stumbled across your cottage in the blizzard. You see – we're lost."

Even to her own ears, Holly's voice sounded forlorn. But as the mystery pony gazed at Holly, his expression softened.

"Ah!" he said. "It's you! I've heard talk of a

young human visitor to Pony Island. The forest sometimes whispers the secrets it has heard on the wind. Well, well, well. How curious!"

Holly saw the pony was now looking intrigued rather than angry, so she seized her moment. "My name's Holly, and this is my friend, Puck. Is there any chance that we could possibly come inside? We've come a long way and we're both very cold. We won't disturb you for long, I promise. We're only looking for shelter."

The mystery pony frowned, and muttered something about not being able to get any peace and quiet these days. But as he pushed open his front door and heaved himself inside, he turned back to look at them expectantly.

“Come on then,” he said gruffly. “Don’t hang about.”

“Thank you!” said Puck, finding his voice again as he trotted in through the open door, heading straight for the little fire burning on the hearth. Holly gazed around the inside of the cottage, thinking how wonderfully warm and snug it looked.

The old pony kneeled down, dropping the wood onto the floor and then piling it piece by piece onto the merrily burning fire.

“I expect you’d both like a hot drink,” he grumbled. Without waiting for an answer, he whispered a spell under his breath and produced two bowls of golden, bubbling liquid.

As Holly sipped it she felt warmth flood through her, tingling all the way to her toes.

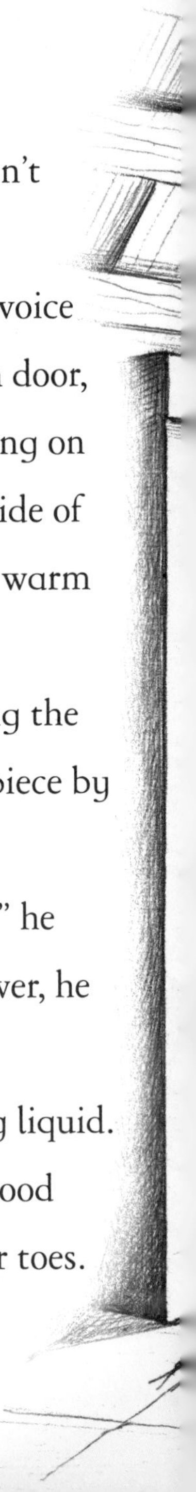

Puck was guzzling his in noisy gulps and he looked up from his empty bowl with a grin,

the mischievous twinkle back in his eyes.

"That was amazing!" he said. "I've never tasted anything like it. What is it?"

"An old recipe," replied the pony. "They probably don't make it like that any more. In my day we called it honey mead."

He began toasting chestnuts over the fire, passing them to Puck and Holly once they were roasted. He broke open the hard cases for Holly with his teeth, so she could scoop out the soft sweet flesh inside.

"Now answer my question," said the pony, once he could see they were warm and fed. "What *are* you doing here? I've never seen weather like this on Pony Island. What's going on?"

"We're looking for Shadow," said Puck, almost gabbling in his desire to explain. "He's an evil pony who wants to take over Pony Island. He told the Pony Queen to give up her powers or he'd open the Cloudburst Casket."

Holly noticed that the old pony looked very grave when Puck mentioned the casket, but he said nothing.

"And that's exactly what he did," Puck went on. "Now Pony Island is covered in darkness. The Pony Queen and the Spell-Keepers are trying to stop the magic of the casket before nightfall, but they don't know how!"

The old pony stood in silence for a few moments longer, his eyes gazing into the distance, as if he were trying to remember something. Puck tried to wait patiently for him to speak again, but he was bursting with curiosity. "Now we've told you everything, won't you tell us who you are?"

"Humph," said the pony. "I thought it wouldn't be long before you asked me that. I can see you're a nosy one."

He cleared his throat. "Well – I suppose there's no harm in telling you. My name is Izagard, not that I expect that to mean anything to you. I am the last in a long line of wizard ponies."

"Wow!" cried Puck. "A wizard pony! I

thought they only existed in legends."

"Like the Cloudburst Casket, you mean?" said Izagard wryly. "No, we wizard ponies exist all right, just like the old magic. But as I grew older, I got tired of always being called upon to work ancient magic for you young ponies, and I came up here, to the High Mountains, to live in peace – until you two came along, that is. Not even the Pony Queen knows I'm here."

"Does that mean," asked Holly, "that you know about the casket? Would you be able to stop it?"

"I'm not sure," said Izagard, shaking his silvery head. "The Cloudburst Casket contains some of the oldest, darkest and most powerful magic on the island. It may be too strong for me to take on – and it's a long time since I tested my powers like that."

He thought for a moment then turned around, so he was gazing into the fire, avoiding their eyes.

"I'm afraid it might be too much for me now," he said finally.

Oh no, thought Holly, her heart sinking. *If Izagard can't help us, how will we* ever *stop Shadow?*

Chapter Six

Holly walked over to Izagard. She had to persuade him to help them. He was their only chance.

"Please, just try," she begged. "For the sake of Pony Island. Have you forgotten how beautiful it is? The Singing River, the Everlasting Rainbow, the flower-filled meadows... It will all be covered in darkness soon. If you help us this once, we'll leave you in peace and never bother you again, I promise."

Puck looked pleadingly at Izagard. "You're our only hope," he added.

Izagard gave a deep sigh. "Very well," he said at last. "I'll agree to help you – on one condition. You must never tell *anyone* about me."

Puck and Holly exchanged glances. They both knew they would be questioned on their return, but they couldn't afford to lose Izagard's help. A flicker of understanding passed between them.

"We promise," Puck and Holly chanted together, both sounding relieved.

Holly saw a glimmer of hope in Puck's eyes. *Perhaps we'll be able to stop Shadow, after all,* she thought.

"Now let me think," said Izagard, frowning. "It's a long time since I've even thought about that casket. It's wooden isn't it, and dark?"

"Yes," said Puck quickly. "And it had strange lines all over it..."

"Almost like cobwebs!" added Holly.

"Yes, that's it!" cried Izagard. "With a spider in the middle. Now I remember. Spiders were used a lot in the old magic. Their webs are incredibly powerful. They can be used to trap all manner of bad spells, including magic storms..."

He stopped speaking, lost in a train of thought, and wandered over to his bookshelves, which were lined with faded spell books. He nosed through one, then muttered, "Ah, yes – the spider's web is the key to controlling the casket."

He turned back to look at Puck and Holly, his eyes lit with a brilliant glow, as if memories of the old magic were flooding back to him. “Now, if I remember rightly, you have until the sun sets to reverse the casket’s magic. So if we’re going to stop it, we will have to act fast.”

“What can we do to help?” Puck asked eagerly, as Izagard began pulling down more spell books from his shelf.

“Go outside,” Izagard replied. “I want you to collect, now let me see…eight small fir twigs and two stones. That should do it. Then hurry back here.”

Puck and Holly raced outside, bracing themselves against the swirling blizzard.

“Do you think he knows what he’s doing?” asked Puck. “It seems like a very odd request. I don’t see how sticks and stones are going to stop the casket.”

"We'll just have to trust him," said Holly, peering through the gloom as she searched for stones in the snow. She realized with a pang of fear how dark it was now. It didn't look like they had much time left.

Puck scooped up a couple of sticks and they headed back inside, where Izagard was waiting for them.

"Well done," he said. "Now lay the stones and twigs down here," he added, indicating a small table near the fire, "and put them all in a pile."

When everything was arranged, Izagard bent low over the table and sprinkled the twigs and stones with a strange, glittering dust.

"Ancient magic dust," he told them, "ground from sunstones and the eggshells of a phoenix."

Then, closing his eyes in concentration, he began chanting a spell in his deep, rumbling voice:

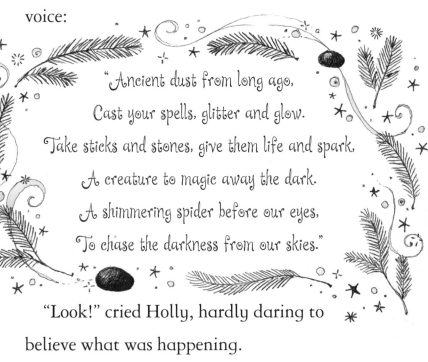

"Ancient dust from long ago,
Cast your spells, glitter and glow.
Take sticks and stones, give them life and spark,
A creature to magic away the dark.
A shimmering spider before our eyes,
To chase the darkness from our skies."

"Look!" cried Holly, hardly daring to believe what was happening.

As Izagard said the words of the spell, the

sticks and the stones were joining together – the twigs forming eight legs that tapped the surface of the table, the shiny black pebbles transformed into a gleaming spider's body.

And as Izagard blew over it, it was as if he were giving it the breath of life. The spider began scurrying back and forth, this way and that, as if desperately searching for something.

"There you go," said Izagard, looking down proudly at the tiny spider.

"But what do we do with it?" asked Holly.

"Take the spider to the casket," said Izagard. "If the magic works, then the spider will know what to do. But hurry! You must leave now, and fly as quickly as you can." He peered anxiously out of his window. "Behind these dark clouds, the sun will soon be setting in the sky – and once it sets, there is no way to reverse the casket's work."

As Holly carefully picked up the spider, Puck headed over to the door. "Thank you for all your help," he said. "We'll never reveal your secret."

"Wait!" Izagard replied. "One more spell is needed before you go. We can't afford for you to get lost on your way to Rainbow Shore, Puck."

He trotted over to them and whispered:

"Wings fly steady, swift and sure,
Straight and true to Rainbow Shore."

"Now you won't get lost, even in the darkest clouds," Izagard explained. "Your wings will know where to take you."

"Thank you," said Puck. Holly leaped quickly onto Puck's back and they galloped out of the little hut and into the swirling snow.

"Goodbye..." called Holly, even as her

voice was whisked away by the wind. She had one last glimpse of Izagard standing by his door, watching them, and then the blizzard blocked her view.

Chapter Seven

Puck flew hard and fast as they left the forest, swooping down through the black storm clouds, anxious to get back to the casket in time.

At last, Rainbow Shore came into view, the rainbow itself shrouded in heavy cloud. The Pony Queen and the Spell-Keepers stood on the beach, with their backs to them. Puck could see books of ancient magic scattered around their feet.

"Where's the casket?" asked Holly.

"There it is!" cried Puck. "Just beyond the Pony Queen."

They landed behind the Spell-Keepers, eager to tell the Pony Queen about the spider. Suddenly, three dark shapes plunged out from one of the blackest clouds and swooped down to the ground. Holly recognized Shadow and his two henchmen. They trampled the spell books into the sand as they landed in front of the Pony Queen.

"It's too late," Shadow announced triumphantly. "The sunshine of Pony Island has been destroyed. In a moment, it will be locked away for ever."

Behind him, the sun peeked out from behind the clouds, its golden disc about to sink into the sea.

"It's *not* too late," cried Holly. "We've found a way to stop the casket!"

Everyone turned to see Holly, sitting astride Puck, the spider held in her outstretched hand.

It shimmered and sparkled in the gloom, casting out a faint ray of light.

Puck looked at Shadow, pleased to see his face grow rigid with shock. It only lasted a moment though, before his expression turned to fury. Then he charged, his hoofs sending up a spray of sand as he came at Puck and Holly, his eyes filled with rage.

Puck tried to back away, but Shadow lunged for Holly, snapping his teeth at the spider in her hand. Puck reared up and Holly seized the moment to throw the spider towards the casket, desperately hoping that Izagard was right and that the spider would know what to do.

But the spider fell to the ground, just short of the casket.

"Oh no!" cried Holly.

Quick as a flash, Shadow lunged after the spider, and Holly watched, horrified, as it disappeared in the sand beneath Shadow's hoofs.

"You've crushed it!" she shouted. "It's all over. You've destroyed Pony Island!"

Shadow's triumphant smile brought tears to Holly's eyes.

But, just then, something began to sparkle and glitter, reminding Holly of the ancient magic dust Izagard had used in his spell. It was the spider! There it was, a little way from Shadow, scuttling over to the casket! Its magic must have protected it from Shadow's pounding hoofs.

Now, surrounded by an intense glow of

light, it scrambled across the lid of the casket like a burnished, dancing sunbeam. As it reached the middle, there was a burst of rainbow light, like a hundred fireworks going off at once. The spider danced around in circles, spinning a golden web with dazzling speed. The web grew before their eyes, huge and glistening in the fading light.

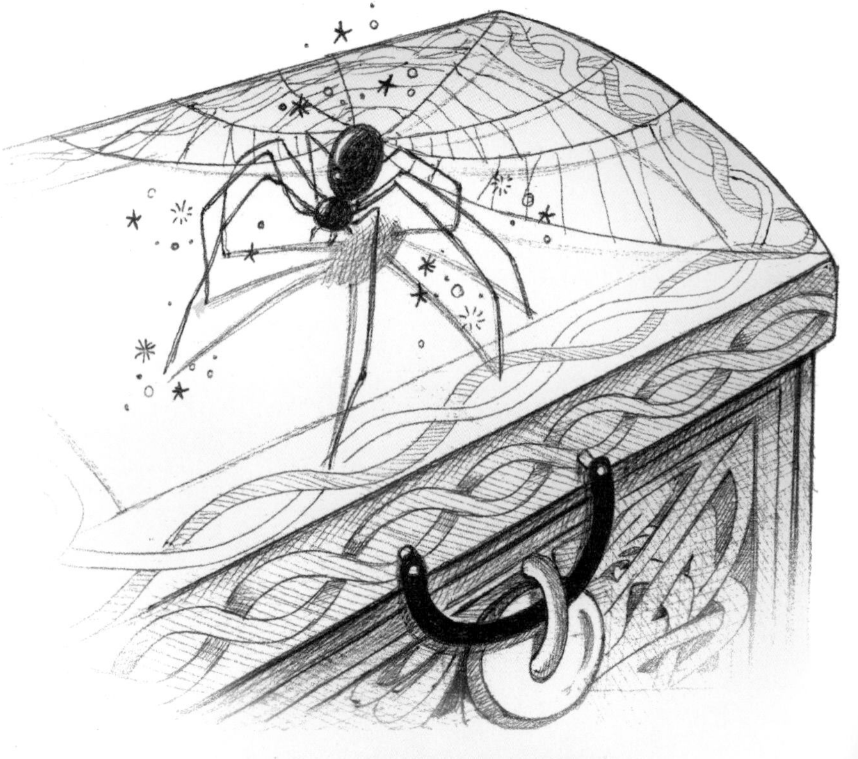

Shadow turned to Storm and Ravenstar, his face glowering with rage.

"It's over. Our plans are in ruins," he snapped. "But this isn't the last of us – Pony Island will be mine!"

Quickly, the three ponies took to the sky. The Spell-Keepers made to go after them, but the Pony Queen called them back.

"There isn't time," she said. "The sun is about to set. Everyone take a piece of the web! That's what the spell books say. We must use the web to catch the clouds."

The Spell-Keepers came together, until they each held a strand of the web.

Puck grabbed a piece between his teeth and Holly took a corner of the silken web with one hand, and jumped onto Puck's back. Then they soared into the sky, the ever-growing web trailing behind them like a vast golden net.

As the web swept across the sky, it gathered up the storm. For a moment,

the web enveloped the clouds in its golden mesh, before they magically faded away.

"Look!" gasped Holly.

As the storm clouds cleared, the sky was lit a brilliant pink by the last rays of the setting sun, and below them, the Everlasting Rainbow was revealed once more, shimmering and sparkling in the sunset, flooding Pony Island with its light.

"I don't think I've ever seen Pony Island look so beautiful," said Holly. She glanced back to see the web vanish, leaving only a golden haze hovering in the air. One by one, the fairy ponies fluttered back down to the ground. Holly could feel a warm breeze blowing in from Rainbow Shore, a sign that the casket's evil magic was truly over.

"We've done it! We've done it!" cheered Puck, his hoofs dancing on the ground. But Bluebell was looking furious.

"I told you both to go home," she said. "How could you put yourselves in such danger?" She shook her head, her face awash with worry.

"It's over now, Bluebell," said the Pony Queen, coming towards them. "And without Holly and Puck's help, we would never have saved Pony Island." As she spoke, the Pony Queen looked closely at them both. Holly held her breath, waiting for her to ask about the spider. But she said nothing. She just smiled a secret smile.

"What about the Rainbow Races?" Puck asked anxiously.

"We'll hold them tomorrow," the Pony Queen announced. "Now we've defeated Shadow, we've got even more to celebrate…"

Chapter Eight

Holly stood beneath the sparkling rainbow, listening to the fanfare from the Fairy Pony Band as the Pony Queen announced the last event of the Rainbow Races. There was no sign now of the havoc and destruction wreaked by the casket. Instead, pretty banners fluttered in the warm breeze and a calm sea glittered beneath the summer sun.

Holly and Puck had had an amazing day. They watched a helter-skelter chase through the sky and a fast and furious race between the Spell-Keepers, from one end of the rainbow to the other. Between the races, they wandered around the brightly decked stalls. There were games of skittles, maypole dancing, flower displays and ponies jumping through fiery hoops. Best of all, Holly thought, were the food stalls, offering honeydew juice, berry cakes, fruit-filled tarts, and rainbow drops that fizzed and popped on her tongue.

"Quick, Holly!" called Puck. "The Juniors race is about to begin."

Puck's butterfly wings were quivering with excitement as they joined his friends at the starting line. Holly swung herself onto Puck's back and wrapped her arms around his neck. Dancer, one of the Spell-Keepers, blew on a seashell horn and they were off, flying in and out of the ribboned masts and then soaring up into the sky as they looped-the-loop above the sand dunes.

"Come on, Puck," shouted Holly, her hair streaming behind her in the breeze as they zoomed their way around a giant conch shell that had been planted in the sand.

They were tearing up through the ranks, in third place now, and Holly found herself whooping with excitement. The air seemed to be alive with fluttering fairy pony wings, delicate yet strong, glittering like a dancing rainbow of light.

Puck flew fast and low as they skimmed the surface of the sea in their race to the sand palace. Holly held her breath as they streamed out on the other side. "We're in second place!" she realized. Only Puck's friend Dandelion was ahead of them now.

For a moment Puck and Holly took the lead, but as they neared the rainbow, Dandelion surged ahead, just reaching the rainbow finishing line before them.

"What a great race!" said Puck, knocking hoofs with Dandelion to congratulate her.

Bluebell clapped and cheered. "Well done, both of you," she said, smiling proudly.

"I wish we'd won, though," said Puck after Dandelion had gone. "We were so nearly there."

Holly stroked his silky mane. "You must still be exhausted from yesterday," she said. "And you did something far more important than win the race – you helped defeat Shadow."

"You're right," said Puck, his face lighting up in a grin. "We saved Pony Island."

As the Rainbow Races drew to a close, Holly and the fairy ponies ran down to the sea for a final frolic in the sun-warmed waves.

"It's nearly time for me to go," she sighed, gazing out across the clear blue sea, as the ponies splashed and played around her.

"I'll fly you home," said Puck. "But promise me you'll come again soon."

"Of course I will," said Holly, throwing her arms around him. "I can't wait for us to have more magical adventures."

Enter the world of the

Fairy Ponies

and collect every enchanting tale

Midnight Escape

Holly is staying with her Great-Aunt May when she discovers a tiny pony with shimmering wings. At first she thinks she must be dreaming...until two fairy ponies visit her with an urgent mission.

ISBN: 9781409506287

Magic Necklace

Holly and her friend Puck are visiting the Pony Queen when a magical necklace is stolen from the palace. Can Puck and Holly help track it down before the thief uses its magic?

ISBN: 9781409506294

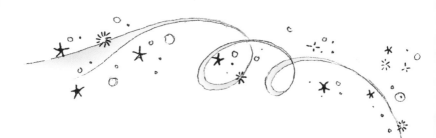

Rainbow Races

Holly can't wait to watch her friend Puck compete in the Rainbow Races – the biggest event on Pony Island. But when an enchanted storm is unleashed, ruining the races, the home of the fairy ponies is threatened with darkness for ever...

ISBN: 9781409506300

Pony Princess

When the Fairy Pony Princess comes to visit, Puck and Holly are given the all-important job of looking after her. But Pony Island is thrown into panic when their royal guest vanishes. Can Puck and Holly find the missing princess?

ISBN: 9781409506379

Coming soon...

Unicorn Prince

When Holly and her fairy pony friend, Puck, uncover a wicked plot to take over Pony Island, their search for the culprit leads them into the mysterious Enchanted Wood, home of the unicorns...

ISBN: 9781409506362

Enchanted Mirror

Pony Island is in danger. The fairy ponies are losing their magic and even the Pony Queen's powers are under threat. Can Holly and Puck uncover the mystery of the missing magic, before it's too late?

ISBN: 9781409506386

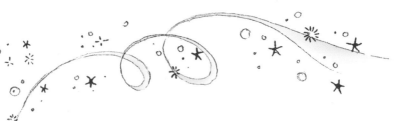

Edited by Stephanie King and Becky Walker

Designed by Brenda Cole

Reading consultant: Alison Kelly,
University of Roehampton

First published in 2014 by Usborne Publishing Ltd.,
Usborne House, 83-85 Saffron Hill, London EC1N 8RT, England.
www.usborne.com

Cover and inside illustrations by Barbara Bongini

A CIP catalogue record for this book is available from the British Library.